KU-033-863

The FiRST EGG HUNT

Adam & **Charlotte Guillain**
Pippa Curnick

DEAN

"It's very nearly **Easter**,"
Bunny said to his friend, Chick.
They were working through their list
And checking jobs off with a tick.

"Chocolate bunnies – **tick!**" said Chick.
"And chocolate eggs all packed."

"Our **best eggs** ever!" Bunny said.
"All neatly wrapped and stacked."

Then over moonlit fields
The Easter Bunny took his load,
And started his deliveries
With tiny Mouse and Toad.

Each beaver, bear and badger
Had a chocolate egg or treat.
Bunny made sure **every** creature
Would wake up to something sweet.

Chick gazed out of her window
And she clapped her wings with glee.
"We've worked so hard," she chirruped.
"I can't wait for them to see!"

Then, early in the morning,
Chick was woken by a cheer:
"Hurray for Easter Bunny!
He brings chocolate every year!"

The woodland creatures cried with joy,

"It's Bunny's best year yet!"

EASTER HQ

"But *I* did half the work," sniffed Chick. "Did everyone forget?"

Soon fan mail started flooding in –

Now Bunny was a **star!**

They put him in a movie
And he bought a

shiny car

Chick stomped away and grumbled,
"Why does **he** get all the fuss?
I'll hatch a plan to show their treats
Have come from **both** of us!"

A year passed, making eggs and
Checking jobs off with a **tick**,
But *this* time Chick popped labels
On each egg signed,

"Love from Chick."

To Do
• wrap eggs ✓
• curl ribbons ✓
• pack eggs ✓
• hang decorations ✓
• refill chocolate ✓
• clean the house ✓
• Brush feathers ✓
• water plants ✓
• Count the buttons ✓
• Post letters ✓
• Polish beak ✓
• Bake Easter cake ✓
• Go to gym

"Chocolate bunnies – **tick!**" said Chick.
"And chocolate eggs all packed."
"Our **best eggs** ever!" Bunny said.
"All neatly wrapped and stacked."

"We're early," simpered crafty Chick –
And laid her cunning trap . . .
"Why don't you have a well-earned rest
And take a **little nap?**"

Then as the sun was setting,
While the Easter Bunny slept,
Chick filled the trolley up with eggs
And out the door she crept!

She trudged across the field with eggs
For tiny Mouse and Toad,

Then hauled her load up Badger's Hill . . .

. . . But tripped up in the road!

"Oh, no!" Chick chirped in panic,
As the eggs rolled down the slope.

She chased the speeding trolley
And she tried to grab the rope.

Then,
BANG!

The trolley hit a rock
And flew up in the air.

"Oh, goodness!" poor Chick whimpered

As the eggs fell . . .

EVERY

Eggs landed in the bushes
And inside a hollow tree.

Chick panicked, **"I can't find them!
It's too dark and I can't see!"**

And when at last the sun rose
At the start of Easter Day,

The creatures
started waking up –

So Chick
just ran away.

Back home, the Easter Bunny stretched
And jumped out of his bed.
"Oh, no! I've overslept!" he cried,
Then frowned and scratched his head.

SQUIRTER

EGGMASTER

FRAGILE

THIS WAY UP

Love from
Chick x

He saw the eggs had disappeared
And gave a little wail.

Just then a tearful Chick burst in
And told her sorry tale.

"I wanted them to notice me!
Oh, dear! What have I done?"

She closed her eyes and sobbed –
But then a voice called . . .

"This is fun!"

When Chick and Bunny crept outside
They saw the strangest sight.
The animals were rushing round
And squeaking in delight!

I found one!" cried a little mole.
Me, too!" exclaimed a frog.
A squirrel squealed and pulled an egg
from underneath a log.

When they saw the Easter Bunny
All the creatures gave a cheer:
"Hooray! We think your egg hunt
Is a **brilliant** idea!"

"My idea?" said Bunny.
"Things are not quite as they seem!
It was my friend, the Easter Chick –
We make a **perfect team!**"

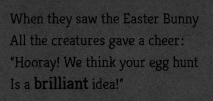

"Three cheers for Chick!" he added
And they roared,

"Hip, hip, hooray!"

Chick beamed and said,
"Let's have an egg hunt . . .